The Great Song Book

Edited by Timothy John
Music edited by Peter Hankey
Illustrated by Tomi Ungerer

Benn Book
COLLECTION

The Benn Book Collection
Published by Doubleday & Company Inc., Garden City, New York

Originally published by Diogenes Verlag Zurich under the title Das Grosse Liederbuch

Edited by Anne Diekmann Text and music Copyright © 1978 Ernest Benn Limited

Copyright for Tomi Ungerer Illustrations © 1975 by Diogenes Verlag AG, Zurich

Benn Book
COLLECTION

Library of Congress Catalog Card Number 77-74707

Library of Congress Cataloging
in Publication Data
The Great Song Book

1. Song books. I. Ungerer, Tomi, 1931-
II. Benn (Ernest) Limited, London.
M1977.C5G747   784.6   77-74707

ISBN 0-385-13328-6

SONGS OF DANCE AND PLAY

Oranges and Lemons

Traditional 18th century words and tune from London

Or - an - ges and le - mons, Say the bells of St. Cle - ment's; You owe me five

far - things, Say the bells of St. Mar - tin's; When will you pay me? Say the

bells of Old Bai - ley; When I grow rich, Say the bells of Shore - ditch; When will that be? Say the

bells of Step - ney; I'm sure I don't know, Says the Great Bell of Bow. Here comes a

can - dle to light you to bed; Here comes a chop-per to chop off your head.

Ring-a-Ring o' Roses

Traditional 17th century words and tune

Ring - a - ring o' ro - ses, a poc - ket full of po - sies, A - ti - shoo! A - ti - shoo! We all fall down.

5

Nuts in May

Traditional 18th century words and tune

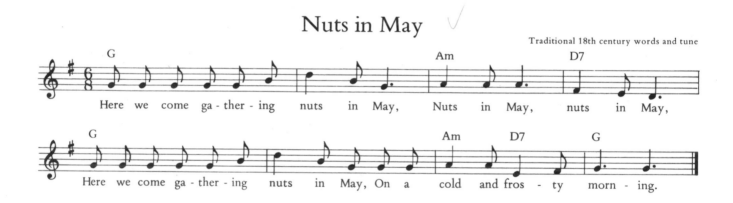

Here we come ga-ther-ing nuts in May, Nuts in May, nuts in May,

Here we come ga-ther-ing nuts in May, On a cold and fros-ty morn-ing.

2. Who will you have for nuts in May,
Nuts in May, nuts in May,
Who will you have for nuts in May,
On a cold and frosty morning?

3. We'll have . . . . . for nuts in May,
Nuts in May, nuts in May,
We'll have . . . . . for nuts in May,
On a cold and frosty morning.

4. Who will you send to fetch him/her away,
Fetch her away, fetch her away,
Who will you send to fetch her away,
On a cold and frosty morning?

5. We'll send . . . . . to fetch him/her away,
Fetch her away, fetch her away,
We'll send . . . . . to fetch her away,
On a cold and frosty morning.

Boys and Girls Come Out to Play

Traditional 18th century words and tune

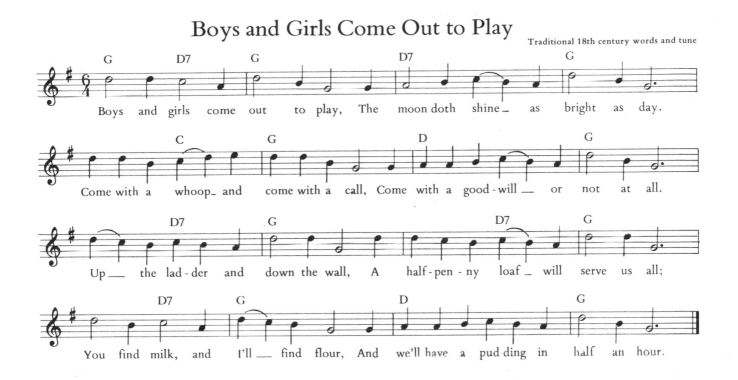

Boys and girls come out to play, The moon doth shine as bright as day.

Come with a whoop and come with a call, Come with a good-will or not at all.

Up the lad-der and down the wall, A half-pen-ny loaf will serve us all;

You find milk, and I'll find flour, And we'll have a pud-ding in half an hour.

7

Here we go Round the Mulberry Bush

Traditional 18th century words and tune

Here we go round the mul - berry bush, The mul - berry bush, the mul - berry bush,

Here we go round the mul - berry bush, On a cold and fros - ty mor - ning.

2. This is the way we wash our hands,
Wash our hands, wash our hands,
This is the way we wash our hands,
On a cold and frosty morning.

3. This is the way we go to school,
Go to school, go to school,
This is the way we go to school,
On a cold and frosty morning.

There's a Hole in my Bucket

Traditional words and tune

There's a hole in my buc-ket, dear Li-za, dear Li-za, there's a hole in my buc-ket, dear Li-za, a hole.

2. Then mend it, dear Henry, dear Henry, dear Henry,
Then mend it, dear Henry, dear Henry, mend it.

3. With what shall I mend it, dear Liza, dear Liza,
With what shall I mend it, dear Liza, with what?

4. With straw, dear Henry, dear Henry, dear Henry,
With straw, dear Henry, dear Henry, with straw.

5. The straw is too long, dear Liza, dear Liza,
The straw is too long, dear Liza, too long.

6. Then cut it, dear Henry, dear Henry, dear Henry,
Then cut it, dear Henry, dear Henry, cut it.

7. With what shall I cut it, dear Liza, dear Liza,
With what shall I cut it, dear Liza, with what?

8. With a knife, dear Henry, dear Henry, dear Henry,
With a knife, dear Henry, dear Henry, a knife.

9. The knife is too blunt, dear Liza, dear Liza,
The knife is too blunt, dear Liza, too blunt.

10. Then sharpen it, dear Henry, dear Henry, dear Henry,
Then sharpen it, dear Henry, dear Henry, sharpen it.

11. With what shall I sharpen it, dear Liza, dear Liza,
With what shall I sharpen it, dear Liza, with what.

12. With a stone, dear Henry, dear Henry, dear Henry,
With a stone, dear Henry, dear Henry, a stone.

13. But the stone is too dry, dear Liza, dear Liza,
But the stone is too dry, dear Liza, too dry.

14. Then wet it, dear Henry, dear Henry, dear Henry,
Then wet it, dear Henry, dear Henry, wet it.

15. With what shall I wet it, dear Liza, dear Liza,
With what shall I wet it, dear Liza, with what.

16. With water, dear Henry, dear Henry, dear Henry,
With water, dear Henry, dear Henry, with water.

17. In what shall I get it, dear Liza, dear Liza,
In what shall I get it, dear Liza, in what?

18. In a bucket, dear Henry, dear Henry, dear Henry,
In a bucket, dear Henry, dear Henry, in a bucket.

19. There's a hole in my bucket, dear Liza, dear Liza,
There's a hole in my bucket, dear Liza, a hole.

NURSERY RHYMES AND SONGS

Lucy Lockett

Traditional 18th century words and tune

Lu - cy Loc - kett lost her poc - ket, Kit - ty Fi - sher found it, But

ne'er a pen - ny was there in it, 'Cept the bin - ding round it.

Lavender's Blue

Traditional 17th century words and tune

Lav - en - der's blue, did - dle, did - dle, lav - en - der's green;

When I am king, did - dle, did - dle, you shall be queen.

2. Call up your men, diddle, diddle, set them to work;
Some to the plough, diddle, diddle, some to the cart.

3. Some to make hay, diddle, diddle, some to cut corn;
Whilst you and I, diddle, diddle, keep ourselves warm.

Hey, Diddle, Diddle

Traditional words and tune

Hey did - dle, did - dle the cat and the fid - dle, The cow jumped ov - er the moon; ___ The lit - tle dog laughed to see such sport, And the dish ran a - way with the spoon.

Hickory, Dickory, Dock

Traditional 17th century words and tune from Westmorland

Hic - ko - ry, dic - ko - ry, dock, ___ The mouse ran up the clock, ___ The clock struck one, the mouse ran down, Hic - ko - ry, dic - ko - ry, dock.

2. Hickory, dickory, dare,
The pig flew in the air.
The man in brown soon brought him down,
Hickory, dickory, dare.

Old King Cole

Traditional 18th century words and tune

Old King Cole was a mer-ry old soul, And a mer-ry old soul was he; He called for his pipe and he called for his bowl, and he called for his fid-dlers three. Ev'-ry fid-dler, he had a fid-dle, a ve-ry fine fid-dle had he; Twee twee did-dle dee, went the fid-dlers three, And so mer-ry we will be!

Goosey, Goosey Gander

Traditional 18th century words and tune

Michael Finnigin

Traditional words and tune

There once was a man named Mi-chael Fin-ni-gin, He grew whis-kers on his chin-ni-gin, The wind came out and blew them in-i-gin, Poor old Mi-chael Fin-ni-gin (be-gin-i-gin).

2. There once was a man named Michael Finnigin,
He kicked up an awful dinigin,
Because they said he must not sinigin,
Poor old Michael Finnigin (beginigin).

3. There once was a man named Michael Finnigin,
He went fishing with a pinigin,
Caught a fish but dropped it inigin,
Poor old Michael Finnigin (beginigin).

4. There once was a man named Michael Finnigin,
Climbed a tree and barked his shinigin,
Took off several yards of skinigin,
Poor old Michael Finnigin (beginigin).

5. There once was a man named Michael Finnigin,
He grew fat and he grew thinigin,
Then he died, and we have to beginigin,
Poor old Michael Finnigin.

Little Boy Blue

Traditional 16th century words and tune

Lit-tle Boy Blue, Come blow your horn, The sheep's in the mea-dow, The cow's in the corn; But where is the boy Who looks af-ter the sheep? He's un-der the hay-cock, Fast a-sleep.

Will you wake him? No, not I, For if I do, He's sure to cry.

Alouette

French Canadian song, French folk tune

A - lou-et - te, gen - tille A - lou-et - te, A - lou et - te, je te plu-me - rai. Je te

plu-me-rai la tête, Je te plu-me-rai la tête, A la tête, à la tête, A - lou - et - te
la bec,   la bec,

repeat as necessary

A - lou-et - te, gen - tille A - lou-et - te, A - lou - et - te, je te plu-me - rai. bec, à le bec, à la
                                                                                    tête, à la tête, A - lou -

1. Alouette, gentille Alouette,
Alouette, je te plumerai.
Je te plumerai le bec,
Je te plumerai le bec,
A le bec, à le bec,
A la tête, à la tête,
Alouette.

2. Alouette, gentille Alouette,
Alouette, je te plumerai.
Je te plumerai les yeux,
Je te plumerai les yeux,
A le bec, à le bec,
A la tête, à la tête,
Alouette.

3. Alouette, gentille Alouette,
Alouette, je te plumerai.
Je te plumerai les ailes,
Je te plumerai les ailes,
A les ailes, à les ailes,
A les yeux, à les yeux,
A le bec, à le bec,
A la tête, à la tête,
Alouette.

4. Alouette, gentille Alouette,
Alouette, je te plumerai.
Je te plumerai le dos,
Je te plumerai le dos,
A le dos, à le dos,
A les ailes, à les ailes,
A les yeux, à les yeux,
A le bec, à le bec,
A la tête, à la tête,
Alouette.

5. Alouette, gentille Alouette,
Alouette, je te plumerai.
Je te plumerai les jambes,
Je te plumerai les jambes,
A les jambes, à les jambes,
A le dos, à le dos,
A les ailes, à les ailes,
A les yeux, à les yeux,
A le bec, à le bec,
A la tête, à la tête,
Alouette.

6. Alouette, gentille Alouette,
Alouette, je te plumerai.
Je te plumerai les pieds,
Je te plumerai les pieds,
A les pieds, a les pieds,
A les jambes, a les jambes,
A le dos, a le dos,
A les ailes, à les ailes,
A les yeux, à les yeux,
A le bec, à le bec,
A la tête, à la tête,
Alouette, gentille Alouette,
Alouette, je te plumerai.

Bobby Shaftoe

Traditional Northumbrian words and tune

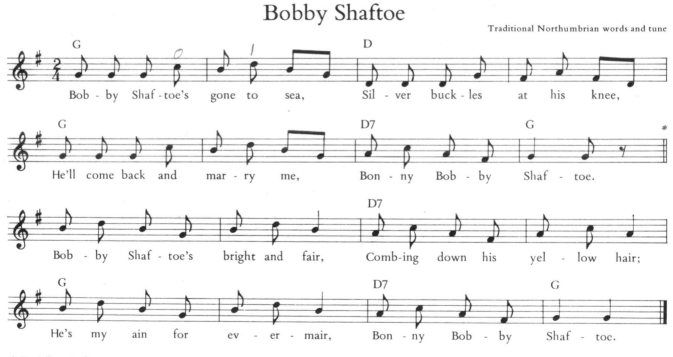

Bob - by Shaf - toe's gone to sea, Sil - ver buck - les at his knee,

He'll come back and mar - ry me, Bon - ny Bob - by Shaf - toe.

Bob - by Shaf - toe's bright and fair, Comb - ing down his yel - low hair;

He's my ain for ev - er - mair, Bon - ny Bob - by Shaf - toe.

End here in last verse

2. Bobby Shaftoe's tall and slim,
Always dressed so neat and trim,
Lassies they all keek at him,
Bonny Bobby Shaftoe.

3. Bobby Shaftoe's getting a bairn,
For to dangle on his airm;
In his airm an' on his knee,
Bonny Bobby Shaftoe.

4. Bobby Shaftoe gone to sea,
Silver buckles at his knee,
He'll come back and marry me,
Bonny Bobby Shaftoe.

Ride a Cock Horse

Traditional 18th century words and tune

Ride a cock horse to Ban-bu-ry Cross, To see a fine la-dy on a white horse;

Rings on her fin-gers and bells on her toes, And she shall have mu-sic where ev-er she goes.

FARMERS' SONGS

The Farmer's in the Dell

Traditional words and tune

The far - mer's in the dell, The far - mer's in the dell, _____

Heigh - oh, the dai - ry oh! The far - mer's in the dell. _____

2. The farmer takes a wife,
The farmer takes a wife,
Heigh-oh, the dairy-oh!
The farmer takes a wife.

3. The wife takes a child,
The wife takes a child,
Heigh-oh, the dairy-oh!
The wife takes a child.

4. The child takes a nurse,
The child takes a nurse,
Heigh-oh, the dairy-oh!
The child takes a nurse.

5. The nurse takes a dog,
The nurse takes a dog,
Heigh-oh, the dairy-oh!
The nurse takes a dog.

6. The dog takes a cat,
The dog takes a cat,
Heigh-oh, the dairy-oh!
The dog takes a cat.

7. The cat takes a rat,
The cat takes a rat,
Heigh-oh, the dairy-oh!
The cat takes a rat.

8. The rat takes the cheese,
The rat takes the cheese,
Heigh-oh, the dairy-oh!
The rat takes the cheese.

9. The cheese stands alone,
The cheese stands alone,
Heigh-oh, the dairy-oh!
The farmer's in the dell.

Aunt Rhody

Traditional words and tune

Go tell Aunt Rho-dy, go tell Aunt Rho-dy, Go tell Aunt Rho-dy, The old gray goose is dead,

2. The one she's been savin', the one she's been savin',
The one she's been savin',
To make a feather bed.

3. She died in the millpond, she died in the millpond,
She died in the millpond,
A-standing on her head.

4. Old Gander's weeping, old Gander's weeping,
Old Gander's weeping,
Because his wife is dead.

5. The goslings are mourning, the goslings are mourning,
The goslings are mourning,
Because their mother's dead.

To be a Farmer's Boy

Traditional 18th century Cornish words and tune

The sun went down beyond yon hill Across the drea-ry moor, When a
And if that you can not me em-ploy, One fa-vour let me ask, Will you

boy there came, both wea-ry and lame, Up to a far-mer's door. "Can you tell me if
shel-ter me till break of day, From this cold win-ter's blast? At the break of day I'll

a-ny there be That can give to me em-ploy? I can plough and sow, and
trudge a-way, And will try to get em-ploy; I can plough and sow, and

reap and mow, And be a far-mer's boy, And be a far-mer's boy.
reap and mow, And be a far-mer's boy, And be a far-mer's boy."

3. The farmer said, "Let stay the lad,
No farther let him seek;"
"Oh yes, dear father," the daughter said,
While the tears ran down her cheek;
"For those that labour, 'tis hard to want,
If that you can give employ,
He can plough and sow, and reap and mow,
And be a farmer's boy,
And be a farmer's boy."

4. The farmer's boy grew up a man,
The good old farmer died,
He left the lad the farm he had,
And the daughter for his bride;
So the lad that was, now a farmer is,
Often smiles and thinks with joy
Of the lucky day he came that way,
To be a farmer's boy,
To be a farmer's boy.

Old MacDonald

Traditional words and tune

Old Mac-Don-ald had a farm, E - I - E - I - O! And on this farm he had some chicks, E - I - E - I - O! With a chick-chick here, and a chick-chick there, Here a chick, there a chick, eve-ry-where a chick-chick.

Old Mac-Don-ald had a farm, E - I - E - I - O! And O!

2. Old MacDonald had a farm,
E-I-E-I-O!
And on this farm he had some turkeys,
E-I-E-I-O!
With a gobble-gobble here, and a gobble-gobble there,
Here a gobble, there a gobble, everywhere a gobble-gobble.
Old MacDonald had a farm,
E-I-E-I-O!

3. Old MacDonald had a farm
E-I-E-I-O!
And on this farm he had some sheep,
E-I-E-I-O!
With a baa-baa here, and a baa-baa there,
Here a baa, there a baa, everywhere a baa-baa,
Old MacDonald had a farm,
E-I-E-I-O!

4. Old MacDonald had a farm,
E-I-E-I-O!
And on this farm he had some cows,
E-I-E-I-O!
With a moo-moo here, and a moo-moo there,
Here a moo, there a moo, everywhere a moo-moo,
Old MacDonald had a farm,
E-I-E-I-O!

5. Old MacDonald had a farm,
E-I-E-I-O!
And on this farm he had some pigs,
E-I-E-I-O!
With a grunt-grunt here, and a grunt-grunt there,
Here a grunt, there a grunt, everywhere a grunt-grunt,
Old MacDonald had a farm,
E-I-E-I-O!

6. Old MacDonald had a farm,
E-I-E-I-O!
And on this farm he had some ducks,
E-I-E-I-O!
With a quack-quack here, and a quack-quack there,
Here a quack, there a quack, everywhere a quack-quack,
Old MacDonald had a farm,
E-I-E-I-O!

The Honest Ploughman

Traditional 19th century words and tune

Come all you jolly husbandmen and listen to my song, I'll relate the life of a ploughman, and not detain you long; My fa-ther was a far-mer, who ba-nished grief and woe; My mo-ther was a dai-ry maid—that's nine-ty years a-go.

2. To drive a plough, my father did a boy engage,
Until that I had just arrived to seven years of age;
So then did he no servant have, my mother milked the cow,
And with the lark I rose each morn to go and drive the plough.

3. When I was fifteen years of age, I used to thrash and sow,
I harrowed, ploughed, and at harvest-time I used to reap and mow;
When I was twenty years of age, I could well manage the farm,
I could hedge and ditch, and plough and sow, or thrash within the barn.

4. When a man has laboured all his life to do his country good,
He's respected just as much when old as a donkey in a wood,
His days are gone and past, and he may weep in grief and woe,
The times are very different now, to ninety years ago.

Pat-a-Cake

Traditional 17th century words and tune

Pat - a - cake, pat - a - cake ba - ker's man,

Bake me a cake as fast as you can. Pat it and prick it, and

mark it with B, Put it in the o - ven for Ba - by and me.

One Man went to Mow

Traditional words and tune

One man went to mow, Went to mow a mea-dow, ___

One man and his dog, Went to mow a mea-dow. ___ Two men went to mow,

Went to mow a mea-dow, _ Two men, one man and his dog, Went to mow a mea-dow. ___

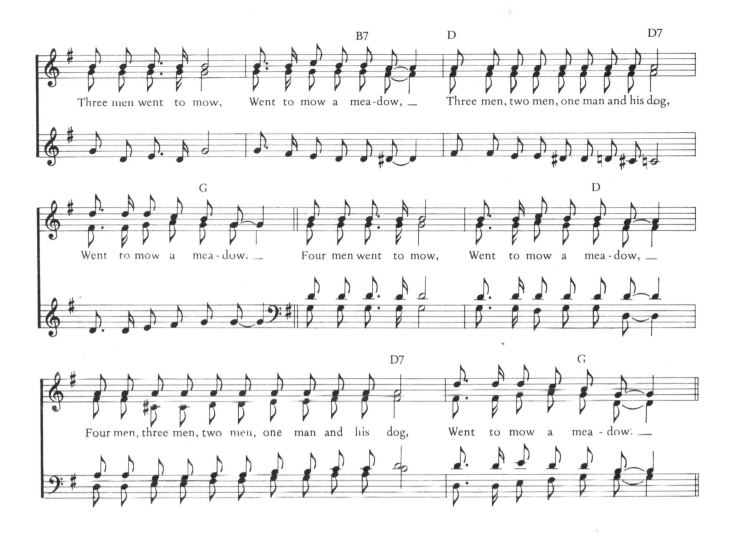

5. Five men went to mow,
Went to mow a meadow,
Five men, four men, three men, two men, one man and his dog,
Went to mow a meadow.

6. Six men went to mow,
Went to mow a meadow,
Six men, five men, four men, three men, two men, one man and his dog,
Went to mow a meadow.

7. Seven men went to mow,
Went to mow a meadow,
Seven men, six men, five men, four men, three men, two men, one man and his dog,
Went to mow a meadow.

8. Eight men went to mow,
Went to mow a meadow,
Eight men, seven men, six men, five men, four men, three men, two men, one man and his dog,
Went to mow a meadow.

MORNING SONGS

Frère Jacques

French folksong

Frè - re Jac - ques, Frè - re Jac - ques, Dor - mez vous? Dor - mez vous? Son-nez les ma - ti - nes, son-nez les ma - ti - nes, Din, din, don, din, din, don.

The Cuckoo

Traditional 18th century words and tune

The cuck - oo is a pret - ty bird, She sings as she flies; She brings us good ti - dings, And tells us no lies.

2. She sucks the pretty flowers
To make her voice clear,
She never says Cuckoo
Till summer is near.

Early One Morning

Traditional words and tune

Ear-ly one morn-ing just as the sun was ris-ing, I heard a maid sing in the val-ley be-low:

"O, don't de-ceive me, O, ne-ver leave me. How could you use a poor mai-den so?"

2. "Remember the vows that you made to me truly,
Remember how tenderly you nestled close to me.
Gay is the garland, fresh are the roses
I've culled from the garden to bind over thee.

3. Here I now wander alone as I wonder
Why you did leave me to sigh and complain.
I ask of the roses, why should I be forsaken,
Why must I in sorrow remain?

4. Through yonder grove, by the spring that is running,
There you and I have so merrily played,
Kissing and courting and gently sporting:
Oh, my innocent heart you've betrayed.

5. How can you slight so a pretty girl that loves you,
A pretty girl that loves you so dearly and warm,
Though love's folly is surely but a fancy,
Still it should prove to me sweeter than your scorn.

6. Soon you will meet with another pretty maiden,
Some pretty maiden, you'll court her for awhile,
Thus ever ranging, turning and changing,
Always seeking for a girl that is new."

7. Thus sang the maiden, her sorrows bewailing,
Thus sang the maid in the valley below:
"O, don't deceive me, O, never leave me,
How could you use a poor maiden so?"

John Peel

Words by John Woodcock Greaves (1820)
Traditional Scottish tune

2. Yes, I ken John Peel and Ruby too,
Ranter and Royal and Bellman as true;
From the drag to the chase, from the chase to a view,
From a view to a death in the morning.
Chorus

3. And I've followed John Peel both often and far
O'er the rasper-fence and the gate and the bar
From Low Denton Holme up to Scratchmere Scar
Where we vied for the brush in the morning.
Chorus

4. Then here's to John Peel with my heart and soul,
Come fill — fill to him another bowl:
And we'll follow John Peel through fair and foul,
While we're waked by his horn in the morning.
Chorus

FIRESIDE SONGS

Cockles and Mussels

Traditional words and old Irish melody

In Dub-lin's fair ci-ty, where the girls are so pret-ty, I first set my eyes on sweet Mol-ly Ma-lone, As she

wheel'd her wheel bar-row through streets broad and nar-row, Crying "Cock-les and mus-sels, a-live, a-live oh! A-

-live, a-live oh ..! A-live, a-live oh!" Crying "Cock-les and mus-sels, a-live, a-live oh!"

2. She was a fishmonger, but sure 'twas no wonder,
For so were her father and mother before;
And they each wheel'd their barrow through their streets broad and narrow,
Crying "Cockles and mussels, alive, alive oh!
    Alive, alive oh! Alive, alive oh!"
    Crying "Cockles and mussels, alive, alive oh!"

3. She died of a fever, and no one could save her,
And that was the end of sweet Molly Malone;
Her ghost wheels her barrow through streets broad and narrow,
Crying "Cockles and mussels, alive, alive oh!
    Alive, alive oh! Alive, alive oh!"
    Crying "Cockles and mussels, alive, alive oh!"

The Drunken Sailor

Traditional sea shanty

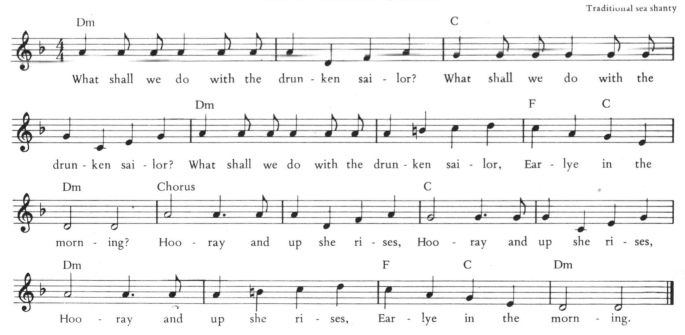

What shall we do with the drun-ken sai - lor? What shall we do with the

drun-ken sai - lor? What shall we do with the drun-ken sai - lor, Ear - lye in the

morn - ing? Hoo - ray and up she ri - ses, Hoo - ray and up she ri - ses,

Hoo - ray and up she ri - ses, Ear - lye in the morn - ing.

2. Put him in the scuppers with a hose-pipe on him,
Put him in the scuppers with a hose-pipe on him,
Put him in the scuppers with a hose-pipe on him,
Earlye in the morning.
  Chorus

3. Take him an' shake him, an' try an' wake him,
Take him an' shake him, an' try an' wake him,
Take him an' shake him, an' try an' wake him,
Earlye in the morning.
  Chorus

47

Clementine

Traditional 19th century American words and tune

In a cav orn, in a can-yon, Ex - ca - va - ting for a mine, Liv'd a min-er for - ty

nin - er, And his daugh - ter Cle-men - tine. Oh my dar-ling, oh my dar-ling, oh my

dar - ling, Cle-men-tine! Thou art lost and gone for ev - er, dread-ful sor - ry, Cle-men-tine.

2. Light she was and like a fairy,
And her shoes were number nine,
Herring boxes without topses,
Sandals were for Clementine.
Chorus

3. Drove her ducklings to the water,
Every morning just at nine,
Hit her foot against a splinter,
Fell into the foaming brine.
Chorus.

4. Saw her lips above the water,
Blowing bubbles mighty fine,
But alas! I was no swimmer,
So I lost my Clementine.
Chorus

5. Then the miner, forty-niner,
Soon began to peak and pine,
Thought he oughta jine his daughter,
Now he's with his Clementine.
Chorus

6. In my dreams she still doth haunt me,
Robed in garlands soaked in brine;
Though in life I used to hug her,
Now she's dead I draw the line.
Chorus

7. How I missed her, how I missed her,
How I missed my Clementine,
But I kissed her little sister,
And forgot my Clementine.
Chorus

Tavern in the Town

Traditional Cornish words and tune

There is a tav-ern in the town, in the town, And there my true love sits him down, sits him down, And drinks his wine 'mid laugh-ter free, And ne-ver ne-ver thinks of me. Fare thee well for I must leave thee, Do not let the par-ting grieve thee, And re--mem-ber that the best of friends must part, must part. A-dieu, a-dieu, kind friends, a-

-dieu, a - dieu, a - dieu. I can no lon - ger stay with you, stay with you, I'll

hang my harp on a weep - ing wil - low tree, And may the world go well with thee.

2. He left me for a damsel dark, damsel dark,
Each Friday night they used to spark, used to spark,
And now my love once true to me,
Takes that dark damsel on his knee.
Fare thee well for I must leave thee,
Do not let the parting grieve thee,
And remember that the best of friends must part, must part.
Adieu, adieu, kind friends, adieu, adieu, adieu.
I can no longer stay with you, stay with you,
I'll hang my harp on a weeping willow tree,
And may the world go well with thee.

3. Oh! Dig my grave both wide and deep, wide and deep,
Put tombstones at my head and feet, head and feet,
And on my breast carve a turtle dove,
To signify I died of love.
Fare thee well for I must leave thee,
Do not let the parting grieve thee,
And remember that the best of friends must part, must part.
Adieu, adieu, kind friends, adieu, adieu, adieu.
I can no longer stay with you, stay with you,
I'll hang my harp on a weeping willow tree,
And may the world go well with thee.

Charlie is my Darling

Traditional Scottish words and tune

2. As he cam' marching up the street,
The pipes play'd loud and clear;
And a' the folks cam' runnin' out,
To meet the chevalier.
Chorus

3. Wi' Hieland bonnets on their heads,
And claymores bright and clear,
They cam' to fight for Scotland's right,
And the young chevalier.
Chorus

4. Oh, there were mony beating hearts,
And mony hopes and fears;
And mony were the pray'rs put up,
For the young chevalier.
Chorus

She'll be Comin'

Traditional American folksong

She'll be com-in' round the moun-tain when she comes, _____ She'll be

com-in' round the moun-tain when she comes, _____ She'll be com-in' round the moun-tain,

com-in' round the moun-tain, She'll be com-in' round the moun-tain when she comes. _____

54

2. She'll be driving six white horses when she comes,
She'll be driving six white horses when she comes,
She'll be driving six white horses, driving six white horses,
She'll be driving six white horses when she comes.

3. O we'll all go to meet her when she comes,
O we'll all go to meet her when she comes,
O we'll all go to meet her, all go to meet her,
O we'll all go to meet her when she comes.

4. And we'll all have chicken and dumplin' when she comes.
And we'll all have chicken and dumplin' when she comes,
And we'll all have chicken and dumplin', all have chicken and dumplin',
And we'll all have chicken and dumplin' when she comes.

The Girl I Left Behind Me

Traditional 18th century words and tune

I'm lone-some since I crossed the hill And o'er the moor and val - ley; Such hea-vy thoughts my heart do fill, Since part-ing with my Sal -ly. I seek no more the fine or gay, For each does but re - mind me How swift the hours did pass a - way With the girl I left be - hind me.

2. Oh! Ne'er shall I forget the night,
The stars were bright above me,
And gently lent their silv'ry light,
When first she vowed to love me.
But now I'm bound to Brighton camp;
Kind heaven, then pray guide me,
And bring me safely back again
To the girl I left behind me.

3. Her golden hair, in ringlets fair,
Her eyes like diamonds shining,
Her slender waist, with carriage chaste,
May leave the swan repining.
Ye gods above! Oh, hear my prayer,
To my beauteous fair to bind me,
And send me safely back again
To the girl I left behind me.

4. I'm lonesome since I cross'd the hill
And o'er the moor and valley;
Such heavy thoughts my heart do fill,
Since parting with my Sally.
I seek no more the fine or gay,
For each does but remind me
How swift the hours did pass away
With the girl I left behind me.

56

Widdicombe Fair

Traditional words and tune from Somerset

Tom Pearce, Tom Pearce, lend me your grey mare; All a-long, down a-long, out a-long lee; For I

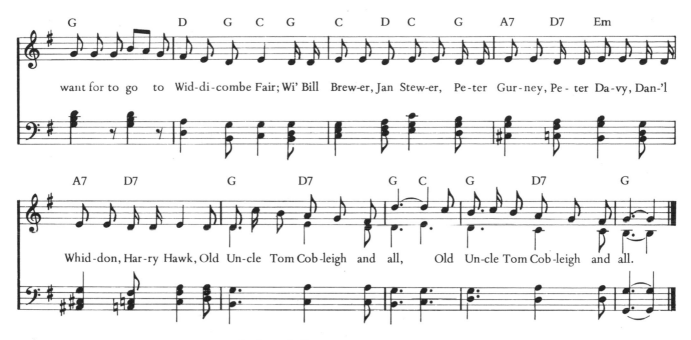

want for to go to Wid-di-combe Fair; Wi' Bill Brew-er, Jan Stew-er, Pe-ter Gur-ney, Pe-ter Da-vy, Dan-'l

Whid-don, Har-ry Hawk, Old Un-cle Tom Cob-leigh and all, Old Un-cle Tom Cob-leigh and all.

2. And when shall I see again my grey mare?
All along, down along, out along lee;
By Friday soon or Saturday noon,
Chorus.

3. Then Friday came and Saturday noon;
All along, down along, out along lee;
Tom Pearce's old mare hath not trotted home,
Chorus.

4. So Tom Pearce, he got to the top of the hill;
All along, down along, out along lee;
And he see'd his old mare down a-making her will,
Chorus.

5. So Tom Pearce's old mare her took sick and died;
All along, down along, out along lee;
And Tom he sat down on a stone and he cried,
Chorus.

6. But this ain't the end o' this shocking affair;
All along, down along, out along lee;
Nor, tho' they be dead, of the horrid career
Of Bill Brewer, Jan Stewer, ...

7. When the wind whistles cold on the moor of a night;
All along, down along, out along lee;
Tom Pearce's old mare doth appear ghastly white,
Chorus.

8. And all the night long be heard skirlings and groans;
All along, down along, out along lee;
From Tom Pearce's old mare in her rattling bones,
Chorus.

Skye Boat Song

Words by Sir Harold Boulton (1884)
Traditional Scottish tune

"Speed, bon-nie boat, like a bird on the wing, On - ward" the sai - lors cry!
"Car - ry the lad that's born to be king O - ver the sea to Skye!"

Loud the winds howl, loud the waves roar, Thun-der clouds rend the air;

Baf - fled our foes stand on the shore, fol - low they will not dare.

2. Though the waves leap, soft shall ye sleep,
Ocean's a royal bed;
Rock'd in the deep, Flora will keep
Watch by your weary head.

"Speed bonnie boat, like a bird on the wing,
Onward," the sailors cry!
"Carry the lad that's born to be king
Over the sea to Skye!"

3. Many's the lad fought on that day,
Well the claymore could wield,
When the night came, silently lay
Dead on Culloden's field.

"Speed bonnie boat, like a bird on the wing,
Onward," the sailors cry!
"Carry the lad that's born to be king
Over the sea to Skye!"

4. Burned are our homes, exile and death
Scatter the loyal men;
Yet, e'er the sword cool in the sheath,
Charlie will come again.

"Speed bonnie boat, like a bird on the wing,
Onward," the sailors cry!
"Carry the lad that's born to be king
Over the sea to Skye!"

Loch Lomond

Traditional Scottish words and tune

By yon bon-nie banks, and by yon bon-nie braes, Where the sun shines bright on Loch Lo - mond, Where

Chorus O ye'll take the high road and I'll take the low road, And I'll be in Scot-land a - fore ye, But

me an' my true love were ev - er wont to gae, On the bon-nie, bon-nie banks of Loch Lo - mond.

me an' my true love will nev-er meet a - gain, On the bon-nie, bon-nie banks of Loch Lo - mond.

2. 'Twas there that we parted in yon shady glen,
On the steep, steep side o' Ben Lomond,
When in purple hue, the Hieland hills we view,
And the moon comin' out in the gloamin'.

O ye'll take the high road and I'll take the low road,
And I'll be in Scotland afore ye,
But me an' my true love will never meet again,
On the bonnie, bonnie banks of Loch Lomond.

3. The wee birdies sing and the wild flowers spring,
And in sunshine the waters lie sleeping;
But the broken heart it kens nae second spring,
Tho' the waefu' may cease frae their greeting.

O ye'll take the high road and I'll take the low road,
And I'll be in Scotland afore ye,
But me an' my true love will never meet again,
On the bonnie, bonnie banks of Loch Lomond.

O, No John

Traditional words and tune from Somerset

2. On her bosom one bunch of posies,
On her breast where flowers grow,
If I should chance to touch that posy,
She must answer yes or no.
O, no, John, no, John, no, John, no.

3. My husband was but a Spanish captain,
Went to sea but a month ago,
And the very last time he kissed and parted
He always bid me answer no.
O, no, John, no, John, no, John, no.

Little Brown Jug

Traditional folksong

My wife and I lived all a-lone, In a lit-tle log hut we called our own. She loved gin and I loved rum. I tell you we had lots of fun! Ha, ha, ha, you and me, Lit-tle brown jug, don't I love thee! Ha, ha, ha, you and me, Lit-tle brown jug, don't I love thee.

2. When I go toiling on my farm
Little brown jug is under my arm.
I place it under a shady tree.
Little brown jug, 'tis you and me.
Chorus

3. My wife and I and a stump-tailed dog
Crossed a creek on a hickory log.
The log did break and we all fell in.
You bet I hung to my jug of gin!
Chorus

4. If I had a cow that gave such milk
I'd dress her in the finest silk,
I'd feed her on the finest hay
And milk her forty times a day!
Chorus

Billy Boy

Traditional English shanty

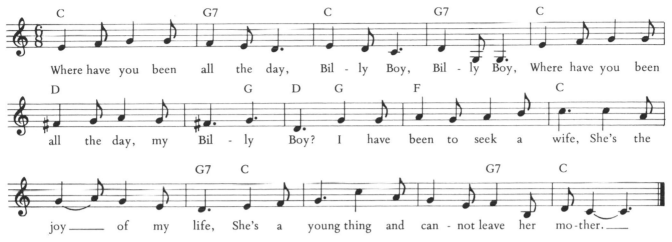

Where have you been all the day, Bil - ly Boy, Bil - ly Boy, Where have you been all the day, my Bil - ly Boy? I have been to seek a wife, She's the joy ____ of my life, She's a young thing and can - not leave her mo - ther. ____

2. Did she ask you to come in, Billy Boy, Billy Boy,
Did she ask you to come in, my Billy Boy?
She did ask me to come in,
She'd a dimple in her chin,
She's a young thing and cannot leave her mother.

3. How old is she, Billy Boy, Billy Boy,
How old is she, my Billy Boy?
She's twice six, twice seven,
Twice twenty and eleven,
She's a young thing and cannot leave her mother.

FOLK SONGS

The Miller of the Dee

Traditional 18th century Scottish words and tune

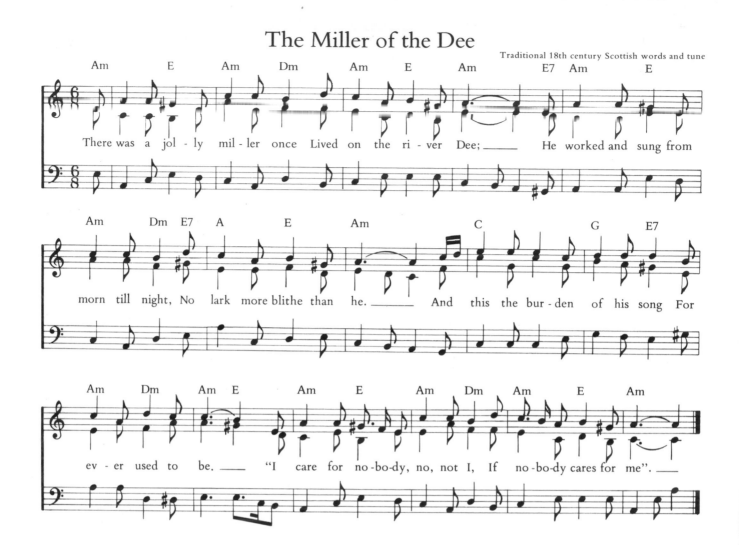

There was a jol - ly mil - ler once Lived on the ri - ver Dee; ___ He worked and sung from morn till night, No lark more blithe than he. ___ And this the bur - den of his song For ev - er used to be. ___ "I care for no - bo - dy, no, not I, If no - bo - dy cares for me". ___

2. I love my mill, she is to me
Like parent, child and wife;
I would not change my station
For any other in life.
No lawyer, surgeon or doctor,
E'er had a groat from me—
And I care for nobody, no, not I,
If nobody cares for me.

The Ash Grove

Words by Thomas Oliphant
Old Welsh tune

2. Still glows the bright sunshine o'er valley and mountain,
Still warbles the blackbird its note from the tree;
Still trembles the moonbeam on streamlet and fountain,
But what are the beauties of nature to me?
With sorrow, deep sorrow, my bosom is laden,
All day I go mourning in search of my love;
Ye echoes! Oh tell me, where is the sweet maiden?
"She sleeps 'neath the green turf sown by the Ash Grove."

Barbara Allen

Traditional words and tune

In Scar-let Town, where I was born, there was a fair maid dwel-lin'; Made ev-'ry youth cry, well-a-day! Her name was Bar-bara Al-len.

2. All in the merry month of May,
When green buds they were swellin';
Young Jemmy Grove on his death-bed lay,
For love of Barbara Allen.

3. He sent his man unto her then,
To the town where she was dwellin';
You must come to my master dear,
If your name be Barbara Allen.

4. So slowly, slowly, she came up,
And slowly she came nigh him;
And all she said, when there she came,
"Young man, I think you're dying.

5. If on your death-bed you do lie,
What needs the tale you're tellin';
I cannot keep you from your death;
Farewell," said Barbara Allen.

6. He turned his face unto the wall,
As deadly pangs he fell in:
"Adieu! Adieu! Adieu to you all,
Adieu to Barbara Allen."

7. As she was walking o'er the fields,
She heard the bell a-knellin';
And every stroke did seem to say,
Unworthy Barbara Allen.

8. When he was dead, and laid in grave,
Her heart was struck with sorrow,
"O mother, mother, make my bed,
For I shall die tomorrow."

9. She, on her death-bed as she lay,
Begg'd to be buried by him;
And sore repented of the day,
That she did e'er deny him.

10. "Farewell," she said, "ye virgins all,
And shun the fault I fell in;
Henceforth take warning of the fall,
Of cruel Barbara Allen."

The Foggy, Foggy Dew

Traditional words and tune

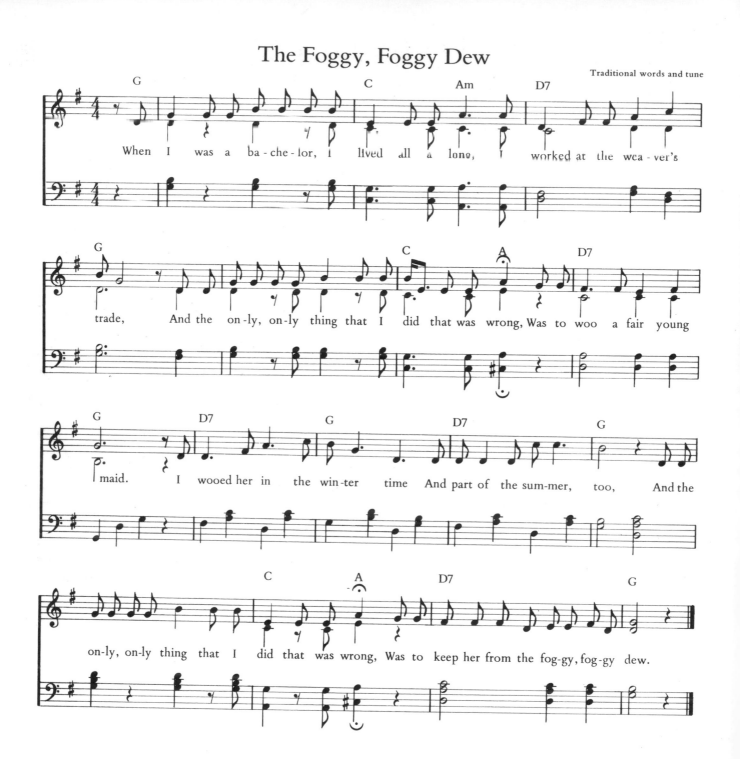

When I was a ba-che-lor, I lived all a-lone, I worked at the wea-ver's trade, And the on-ly, on-ly thing that I did that was wrong, Was to woo a fair young maid. I wooed her in the win-ter time And part of the sum-mer, too, And the on-ly, on-ly thing that I did that was wrong, Was to keep her from the fog-gy, fog-gy dew.

2. One night she came to my bedside,
When I was fast asleep,
She flung her arms around my neck
And then began to weep.
She wept, she cried, she tore her hair,
Ah me, what could I do?
So all night long I held her in my arms,
Just to keep her from the foggy, foggy dew.

3. Still I am a bachelor, I live with my son,
We work at the weaver's trade.
And every time I look into his eyes
He reminds me of that fair young maid.
He reminds me of the wintertime,
And part of summer too,
And of the many, many times I held her in my arms,
Just to keep her from the foggy, foggy dew.

Georgie

Traditional folksong

As I walked out o-ver Lon-don Bridge One mid-sum-mer morn-ing ear - ly, And
there I be-held a fair la - dy, La - men-ting_____ for her Geor-gie.

2. "I pray can you send me a little boy
Who can go an errand swiftly?
Who can go ten miles in one hour
With a letter for a lady."

3. "So come saddle me my best black horse,
Come saddle it quite swiftly,
So I may ride to the King's Castle gaol
And beg for the life of me Georgie."

4. So when she got to the castle door
The prisoners stood many;
They all stood around with their caps in their hands
Excepting her bonny, bonny Georgie.

5. "My Georgie never stole neither horse nor cow,
Not done any harm to any;
He stole sixteen of the King's fat deers
Which grieved me most of any."

6. "Now six pretty babes that are born by him,
The seventh lay at my bosom;
I would freely part with six of them
To spare the life of me Georgie."

7. Now the judge he looked over his left shoulder,
He seemed so very hard-hearted;
He said, "Fair lady, you are too late,
Your Georgie is condemned already."

8. "Now me Georgie shall be hanged in the chains of gold,
Such gold as they don't hang many.
Because he come of the royal blood,
And courted a very rich lady."

9. Now me Georgie shall be hanged in the chains of gold,
Such gold as you don't see any;
And on the tombstone these words should be wrote—
'Here lays the heart of a lady.' "

John Riley

Traditional folksong

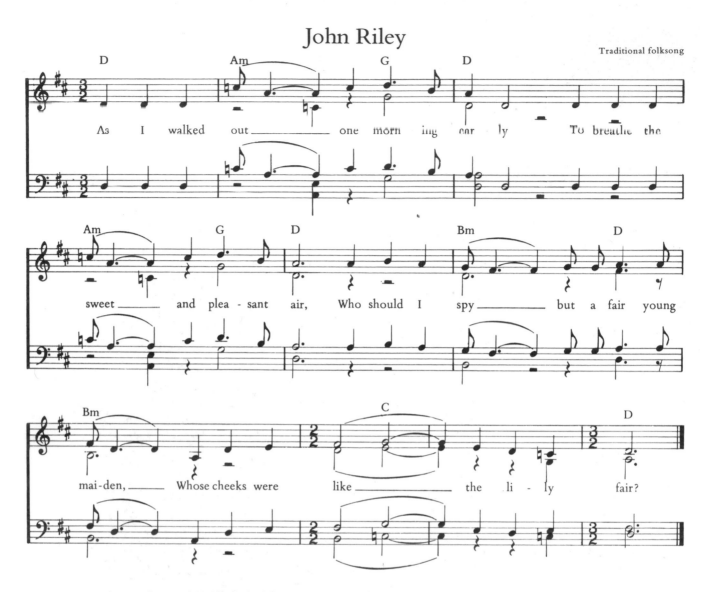

As I walked out one morning early To breathe the sweet and pleasant air, Who should I spy but a fair young maiden, Whose cheeks were like the lily fair?

2. I stepped up to her and kindly asked her
If she would be a sailor's wife.
"O no, kind sir, I'd rather tarry
And remain single for all my life."

3. "What makes you so far from all human nature?
What makes you so far from all human kind?
You are young, you are youthful, fair and handsome,
You can marry me if you're so inclined."

4. "The truth, kind sir, I'll plainly tell you,
I could have married three years ago
To one John Riley who left this country,
Who has been the cause of my grief and woe."

5. "Come along with me, don't think of Riley.
Come, go with me to a distant shore.
We will set sail for Pennsylvany,
Adieu to England for evermore."

6. "I'll not go with you to Pennsylvany,
I'll not go with you to a distant shore;
For my heart is with Riley and I can't forget him,
Although I may never see him no more."

7. Now when he saw that she loved him truly,
He gave her kisses one, two, three,
Saying. "I am Riley, your long-lost lover,
Who has been the cause of your misery."

8. "If you be he and your name be Riley,
I will go with you to that distant shore,
We will set sail for Pennsylvany,
Adieu to England for evermore."

9. They locked their hands and their hearts together
And to the church house they did go,
And they got married to one another,
They're living together, doing well.

The Minstrel Boy

Words by Thomas Moore (1779-1852)
Old Welsh tune

The min-strel boy to the war is gone, In the ranks of death you'll find him, His fa-ther's sword he gir-ded on and his wild harp slung be-hind him. "Land of song," said the war-rior bold, "though all the world be-trays thee, One sword at least thy nights shall guard, one faith-ful harp shall praise thee."

2. The minstrel fell but the foeman's chain
Could not bring his proud soul under;
The harp he lov'd ne'er spoke again, for he tore its chords asunder;
And said, "No chains shall sully thee, thou soul of love and bravery!
Thy sons were made for the pure and free, they shall never sound in slavery!"

80

Tom Dooley

Traditional American words and tune

Oh, hang down your head, Tom Dooley, Oh, hang down your head and cry. You killed poor Laura Foster, And now you are bound to die.

Verses 1 & 2

Last verse

2. You met her on the hillside,
Supposed to be your wife,
You met her on the hillside,
And there you took her life.

A-rovin'

Traditional sea shanty

2. One night I crept from my abode.
Mark well what I do say!
One night I crept from my abode,
To meet this fair maid down the road,
We'll go no more a-rovin' with you fair maid!
Chorus

3. I took this fair maid for a walk.
Mark well what I do say!
I took this fair maid for a walk,
An' we had such a lovin' talk,
We'll go no more a-rovin' with you fair maid!
Chorus

Scarborough Fair

Traditional folksong from North England

G   Am   D   Am   G

"O, where are you go - ing?" "To Scar - bo - rough Fair," Sav - ou - ry,

Am   C   D   G   Am

sage, rose - ma - ry and thyme; "Re - mem - ber me to a

D   Am   F   Am   D   G

lass who lives there, For once she was a true love of mine."

2. And tell her to make me a cambric shirt,"
Savoury, sage, rosemary and thyme;
"Without any seam or needlework,
And then she shall be a true love of mine.

3. And tell her to wash it in yonder dry well,"
Savoury, sage, rosemary and thyme;
"Where no water sprung, nor a drop of rain fell,
And then she shall be a true love of mine.

4. Tell her to dry it on yonder thorn,"
Savoury, sage, rosemary and thyme;
"Which never bore blossom since Adam was born,
And then she shall be a true love of mine."

5. O, will you find me an acre of land,"
Savoury, sage, rosemary and thyme;
"Between the sea foam, the sea sand,
Or never be a true lover of mine.

6. O, will you plough it with a ram's horn,"
Savoury, sage, rosemary and thyme;
"And sow it all over with one peppercorn,
Or never be a true lover of mine.

7. O, will you reap it with a sickle of leather,"
Savoury, sage, rosemary and thyme;
"And tie it all up with a peacock's feather,
Or never be a true lover of mine.

And when you have done and finished your work,"
Savoury, sage, rosemary and thyme;
"You may come to me for your cambric shirt,
And then you shall be a true lover of mine."

CHRISTMAS SONGS

Good King Wenceslas

Words by J. M. Neale (1818–1866)
Traditional tune

Good King Wen-ces-las looked out, On the feast of Ste-phen, When the snow lay
round a-bout, Deep and crisp and e-ven; Bright-ly shone the moon that night,
Though the frost was cru-el, When a poor man came in sight, Gather-ing win-ter fu-el.

2. "Hither, page, and stand by me,
If thou know'st it, telling,
Yonder peasant, who is he?
Where and what his dwelling?"
"Sir, he lives a good league hence,
Underneath the mountain,
Right against the forest fence,
By St. Agnes' fountain."

3. "Bring me flesh and bring me wine,
Bring me pine-logs hither:
Thou and I will see him dine,
When we bear them thither."
Page and monarch forth they went,
Forth they went together;
Through the rude wind's wild lament
And the bitter weather.

4. "Sire, the night is darker now,
And the wind blows stronger;
Fails my heart, I know not how,
I can go no longer."
"Mark my foot steps, good my page;
Tread thou in them boldly:
Thou shalt find the winter's rage
Freeze thy blood less coldly."

5. In his master's steps he trod,
Where the snow lay dinted;
Heat was in the very sod
Which the saint had printed.
Therefore, Christian men, be sure,
Wealth or rank possessing,
Ye who will now bless the poor,
Shall your selves find blessing.

In the Bleak Mid-Winter

Words by Christina Rossetti (1830–94).
Tune, Cranham, by Gustav Holst (1874–1934). From the English Hymnal
by permission of the Oxford University Press.

In the bleak mid - win - ter   Fros - ty wind made moan,

Earth stood hard as i - ron,   Wa-ter like a stone;   Snow had fall - en, snow on snow,

Snow on snow,   In the bleak mid - win - ter.   Long a - go.

2. Our God, heaven cannot hold him,
Nor earth sustain;
Heaven and earth shall flee away
When he comes to reign:
In the bleak mid-winter
A stable-place sufficed
The Lord God Almighty
Jesus Christ.

3. Enough for him, whom Cherubim
Worship night and day,
A breastful of milk,
And a mangerful of hay;
Enough for him, whom Angels
Fall down before,
The ox and ass and camel
Which adore.

4. Angels and Archangels
May have gathered there,
Cherubim and Seraphim
Thronged the air:
But only his mother
In her maiden bliss
Worshipped the belovèd
With a kiss.

5. What can I give him,
Poor as I am?
If I were a shepherd
I would bring a lamb,
If I were a wise man
I would do my part:
Yet what I can I give him—
Give my heart.

Silent Night

Translation Anon.
Tune by Franz Gruber (1838)

Silent night, Holy night, All is calm, all is bright;
'Round yon vir - gin mo-ther and child, Ho - ly In -fant so ten - der and mild,
Sleep in hea - ven -ly peace, _____ Sleep in hea - ven -ly peace.

2. Silent night, Holy night,
Shepherds quake at the sight;
Glories stream from heaven afar,
Heav'nly hosts sing Alleluia!
Christ the Saviour is born!
Christ the Saviour is born!

3. Silent night, Holy night,
Son of God, love's pure light;
Radiance beams from Thy holy face,
With the dawn of redeeming grace,
Jesus, Lord, at Thy birth,
Jesus, Lord, at Thy birth.

Away in a Manger

Words Anon.
Tune by W. J. Kirkpatrick (1838–1921)

A - way in a man - ger, no crib for a bed, The lit - tle Lord Je - sus laid down his sweet head, The stars in the bright sky looked down where he lay, The lit - tle Lord Je - sus a - sleep on the hay.

2. The cattle are lowing, the baby awakes,
But little Lord Jesus no crying he makes.
I love thee, Lord Jesus! Look down from the sky,
And stay by my side until morning is nigh.

3. Be near me, Lord Jesus; I ask thee to stay
Close by me for ever, and love me, I pray.
Bless all the dear children in thy tender care,
And fit us for heaven, to live with thee there.

Joseph, Dearest Joseph Mine

Traditional German carol

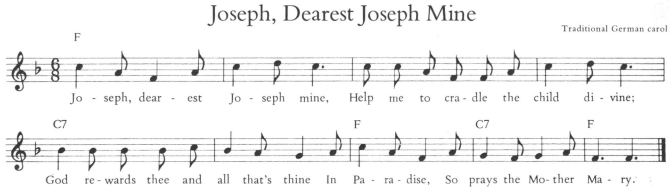

Jo - seph, dear - est Jo - seph mine, Help me to cra - dle the child di - vine;

God re - wards thee and all that's thine In Pa - ra - dise, So prays the Mo- ther Ma - ry.

2. Gladly, dear one, lady mine,
Help I cradle this child of mine;
God's own light on us both shall shine
In Paradise,
As prays the Mother Mary.

While Shepherds Watched

Words by Nahum Tate (1652-1715)
Tune from Este's Psalter 1592

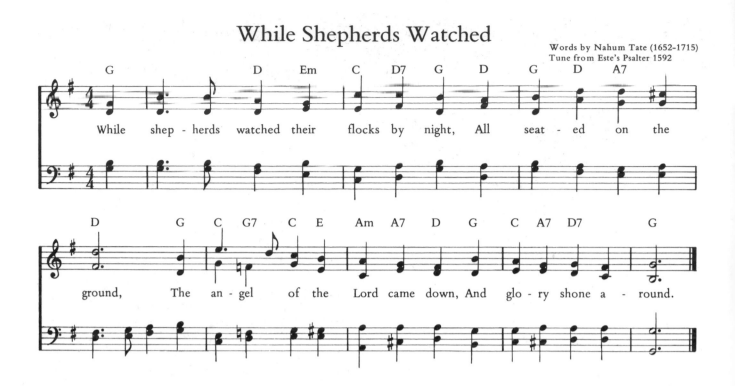

2. "Fear not," said he (for mighty dread
Had seized their troubled minds);
"Glad tidings of great joy I bring
To you and all mankind.

3. To you in David's town this day
Is born of David's line
A Saviour, who is Christ the Lord;
And this shall be the sign:

4. The heavenly babe you there shall find
To human view displayed,
All meanly wrapped in swathing bands,
And in a manger laid."

5. Thus spake the Seraph: and forthwith
Appeared a shining throng
Of angels praising God, who thus
Addressed their joyful song:

6. "All glory be to God on high
And on the earth be peace;
Good will henceforth from heaven to men
Begin and never cease."

Alleluia

Al - le - lu - ia, Al - le - lu - ia, A - men, A - men.

In Dulci Jubilo

Traditional German carol (14th cent.)
Translation by R. L. Pearsall (1837)

In dul - ci ju - bi - lo,_____ Let us our hom - age show,_____ Our heart's

joy re - cli - neth In prae - se - pi - o, _____ And like a bright star shi - neth, Ma-

tris in gre - mi - o _____ Al - pha es et O, _____ Al - pha es et O.

2. O Jesu parvule!
I yearn for thee alway!
Hear me, I beseech thee,
O puer optime!
My prayer let it reach thee,
O princeps gloriae!
Trahe me post te! Trahe me post te!

3. O patris caritas,
O nati lenitas!
Deeply were we stainèd
Per nostra crimina;
But thou hast for us gainèd
Coelorum gaudia.
O that we were there! O that we were there!

4. Ubi sunt gaudia,
If that they be not there?
There are angels singing,
The bells are ringing there
Nova cantica,
There the bells are ringing
In regis curia:
O that we were there! O that we were there!

Ding Dong Merrily on High

Words by G. R. Woodward
16th century French tune

Ding dong! Mer - ri - ly on high In heav'n the bells are ring - ing.
Ding dong! Ve - ri - ly the sky Is riv'n with an - gel sing - ing.

Glo —

— ri - a, Ho - san - na in ex - cel - sis!

2. E'en so there below, below,
Let steeple bells be swungen.
And i-o, i-o, i-o,
By priest and people sungen.
Gloria, Hosanna in excelsis!

3. Pray you, dutifully prime
Your matin chime, ye ringers;
May you beautifully rime
Your evening song, ye singers.
Gloria, Hosanna in excelsis!

A Merry Christmas

Traditional carol from the West Country of England

We wish you a mer-ry Christ-mas, We wish you a mer-ry Christ-mas, We wish you a mer-ry Christ-mas And a hap-py New Year. Good ti-dings we bring To you and your kin; We wish you a mer-ry Christ-mas And a hap-py New Year.

2. Now bring us some figgy pudding,
Now bring us some figgy pudding,
Now bring us some figgy pudding,
And bring some out here.
Chorus

3. For we all like figgy pudding,
For we all like figgy pudding,
For we all like figgy pudding,
So bring some out here.
Chorus

4. And we won't go till we've got some,
And we won't go till we've got some,
And we won't go till we've got some,
So bring some out here.
Chorus

Oh Christmas Tree

Traditional German carol

Oh Christ-mas tree, oh Christ-mas tree, With faith-ful leaves un - chang-ing; Not on-ly green in sum-mer's heat, But al - so win - ter's snow and sleet, Oh Christ-mas tree, oh Christ-mas tree, With faith-ful leaves un - chang-ing.

2. Oh Christmas tree, oh Christmas tree,
Of all the trees most lovely;
Each year, you bring to me delight
Shining bright on Christmas night.
Oh Christmas tree, oh Christmas tree,
Of all the trees most lovely.

3. Oh Christmas tree, oh Christmas tree,
Your leaves will teach me, also,
That hope and love and faithfulness
Are precious things I can possess.
Oh Christmas tree, oh Christmas tree,
Your leaves will teach me also.

The Old Year now Away is Fled

(To the tune Greensleeves)

Traditional tune.
Words adapted by Percy Dearmer from *New Christmas Carols* (1642)
reprinted by kind permission of Oxford University Press.

The old year now a-way is fled, The new year it is en-ter-ed; Then
let us now our sins down-tread, All joy-ful-ly all ap-pear:
Let's mer-ry be this day, And let us now both sport and play:
Hang grief, cast care a-way! God send you a hap-py New Year!

2. The name-day now of Christ we keep,
Who for our sins did often weep;
His hands and feet were wounded deep,
And his blessèd side with a spear;
His head they crowned with thorn,
And at him they did laugh and scorn,
Who for our good was born:
God send us a happy New Year!

3. And now with New Year's gifts each friend
Unto each other they do send:
God grant we may all our lives amend,
And that the truth may appear.
Now, like the snake, your skin
Cast off, of evil thoughts and sin,
And so the year begin:
God send us a happy New Year!

Coventry Carol

15th century English carol

Lul - ly, lul - la, thou lit - tle ti - ny child, By by lul - ly lul -

lay, thou lit - tle ti - ny child, By by, lul - ly lul - lay.

O sis - ters too, How may we do For to pre - serve this day This

poor young - ling, For whom we do sing, By by lul - ly lul - lay.

2. Herod, the king,
In his raging,
Charged he hath this day
His men of might,
In his own sight,
All young children to slay.

3. That woe is me,
Poor child for thee!
And ever morn and day,
For thy parting
Neither say nor sing
By by, lully lullay.

EVENING SONGS

Rock-a-Bye Baby

Traditional 18th century words and tune

Rock-a-bye ba - by on the tree top, When the wind blows the cra - dle will rock.

When the bough breaks the cra - dle will fall And down will come cra - dle, ba - by, and all.

Golden Slumbers

Traditional English lullaby

Gol – den slum – bers kiss your eyes, Smiles a – wait you when you rise;

Sleep pret – ty wan – tons, do not cry, And I will sing a lul – la – by.

2. Care you know not, therefore sleep,
While I o'er you watch do keep,
Sleep, pretty darlings do not cry,
And I will sing a lullaby.

Hush, Little Baby

Traditional words and tune

Hush, lit-tle ba-by, don't say a word Ma-ma's going to buy you a mock-ing bird.

If that mock-ing bird don't sing, Ma-ma's going to buy you a dia-mond ring.

2. If that diamond ring turns brass,
Mama's going to buy a looking glass.

3. If that looking glass gets broke,
Mama's going to buy you a billy goat.

4. If that billy goat won't pull,
Mama's going to buy you a cart and bull.

5. If that cart and bull turn over,
Mama's going to buy you a dog named Rover.

6. If that dog named Rover won't bark,
Mama's going to buy you a horse and cart.

7. If that horse and cart fall down,
You'll still be the prettiest girl in town.

All Through the Night

Words by Sir Harold Boulton (1884)
Old Welsh tune

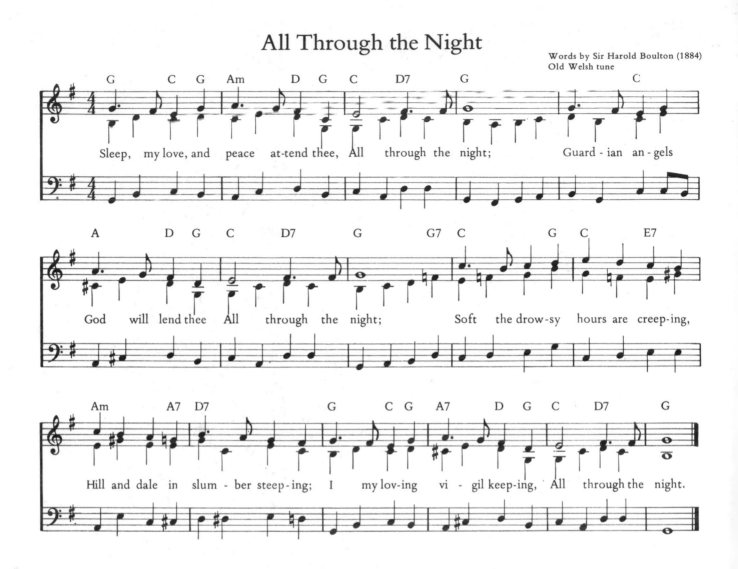

Sleep, my love, and peace at-tend thee, All through the night; Guard - ian an - gels

God will lend thee All through the night; Soft the drow-sy hours are creep-ing,

Hill and dale in slum - ber steep-ing; I my lov-ing vi - gil keep-ing, All through the night.

2. Angels watching ever round thee,
All through the night;
In thy slumbers close surround thee,
All through the night.
They should of all fears disarm thee,
No forebodings should alarm thee,
They will let no peril harm thee,
All through the night.

INDEX